T4-ADM-316

THE TOP SECRET LIFE OF PLANTS

MEAT-EATING PLANTS

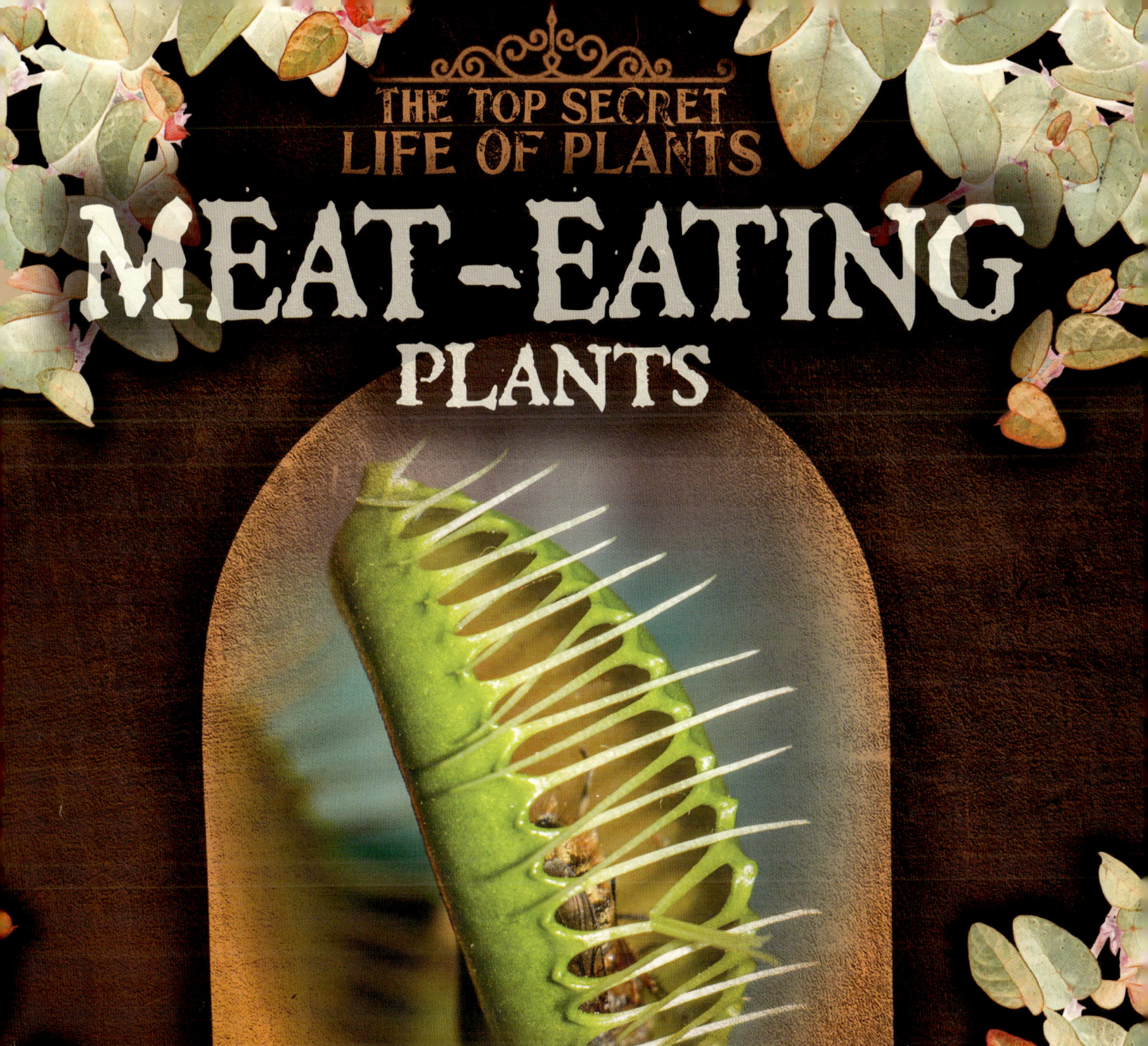

BY SARAH MACHAJEWSKI

Gareth Stevens
PUBLISHING

Please visit our website, www.garethstevens.com. For a free color catalog of all our high-quality books, call toll free 1-800-542-2595 or fax 1-877-542-2596.

Library of Congress Cataloging-in-Publication Data

Names: Machajewski, Sarah, author.
Title: Meat-eating plants / Sarah Machajewski.
Description: New York : Gareth Stevens Press, [2020] | Series: The top secret life of plants | Includes index.
Identifiers: LCCN 2018032238| ISBN 9781538233931 (library bound) | ISBN 9781538233917 (pbk.) | ISBN 9781538233924 (6 pack)
Subjects: LCSH: Carnivorous plants–Juvenile literature.
Classification: LCC QK917 .M2245 2019 | DDC 583/.887–dc23
LC record available at https://lccn.loc.gov/2018032238

First Edition

Published in 2020 by
Gareth Stevens Publishing
111 East 14th Street, Suite 349
New York, NY 10003

Copyright © 2020 Gareth Stevens Publishing

Designer: Sarah Liddell
Editor: Abby Badach Doyle

Photo credits: Cover, p. 1 Natalia Ramirez Roman/Shutterstock.com; glass dome shape used throughout bombybamby/Shutterstock.com; leaves used throughout janniwet/Shutterstock.com; background texture used throughout MInerva Studio/Shutterstock.com; p. 5 Copyright OneliaPG Photography/Moment/Getty Images; p. 7 (regular plant) amenic181/Shutterstock.com; p. 7 (meat-eating plant) Cathy Keifer/Shutterstock.com; p. 9 Matauw/Shutterstock.com; p. 11 nico99/Shutterstock.com; p. 13 Bengal at a glance/Moment Open/Getty Images; p. 15 Kirschner/Shutterstock.com; p. 17 Pierre-Yves Babelon/Moment/Getty Images; p. 19 Luka Hercigonja/Shutterstock.com; p. 21 chakapong/Shutterstock.com.

All rights reserved. No part of this book may be reproduced in any form without permission in writing from the publisher, except by a reviewer.

Printed in the United States of America

CPSIA compliance information: Batch #CS19GS: For further information contact Gareth Stevens, New York, New York at 1-800-542-2595.

CONTENTS

Not So Safe 4
Who's Hungry? 6
The Secrets of Survival 8
Open Wide 10
It's a Trap! 12
Sticky Sundews 14
Pitcher Plants 16
Bladderworts 18
Plants on the Hunt 20
Glossary 22
For More Information 23
Index 24

Words in the glossary appear in **bold** type
the first time they are used in the text.

NOT SO SAFE

From the outside, plants look like they're pretty safe creatures. They can't move. They don't have arms or legs. They don't have a mouth, either. But here's a surprising secret...some plants are deadly predators!

Some plant **species** are known for eating meat. Over time, meat-eating plants have perfected the art of trapping and killing their prey. These hungry hunters work to **attract** and eat bugs, worms, or even small animals such as frogs. How do they do it? Let's find out!

CLASSIFIED!

A PREDATOR IS AN ANIMAL OR PLANT THAT HUNTS OTHER CREATURES FOR PREY. PREY IS A CREATURE HUNTED FOR FOOD.

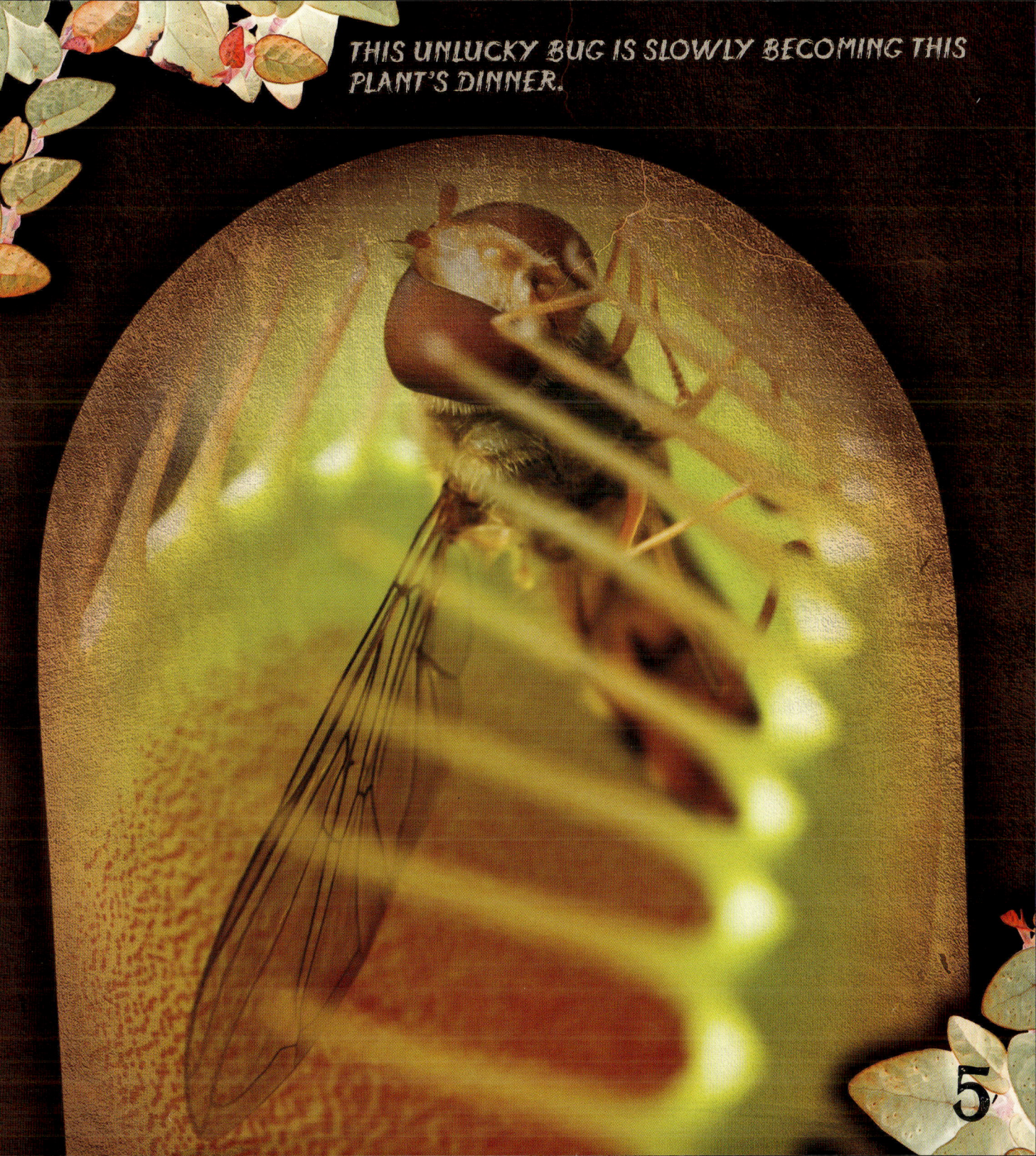

THIS UNLUCKY BUG IS SLOWLY BECOMING THIS PLANT'S DINNER.

5

WHO'S HUNGRY?

Most plants get all the **nutrients** they need to survive from the soil. The nutrients get sucked in through the roots and spread to other parts of the plant to keep it healthy and strong. Meat-eating plants are different. Most live in wet **environments** where nutrients are harder to find.

CLASSIFIED!
MEAT-EATING PLANTS ARE ALSO CALLED INSECTIVORES (IHN-*SEK*-TUH-VORES) OR CARNIVOROUS (KAR-*NIH*-VOR-UHS) PLANTS.

To get enough nutrients, they also eat living prey, like bugs or even small animals. Through a slow process, the plant releases juices that break down the bug's body. Then, the plant **absorbs** the nutrients. Yum!

LOOK AT THE DIFFERENCES BETWEEN MEAT-EATING PLANTS AND REGULAR PLANTS. WHAT DO YOU NOTICE?

REGULAR PLANTS VS. MEAT-EATING PLANTS: WHAT'S DIFFERENT?

	REGULAR PLANTS	MEAT-EATING PLANTS
HOW MANY SPECIES?	about 390,000	between 600-700
FOOD	nutrients from soil	nutrients from soil, and bugs or small animals
HABITAT	just about anywhere with enough sunlight and water	low-nutrient **habitats,** such as bogs and swamps

meat-eating plant ....

.... regular plant

THE SECRETS OF SURVIVAL

Of all the plants living today, not many eat meat. Over time, some plants started to trap bugs and turn them into food. How is it that some plants can do this, but others can't?

When a living thing changes over many years, it's called an adaptation (a-dap-TAY-shun). An adaptation allows plants to better survive in their environment. The ability to "eat" gives meat-eating plants the nutrients they need to stay alive. Without enough food, the plant could die.

CLASSIFIED!

ADAPTATIONS ARE PASSED ON TO NEW PLANTS OVER TIME, UNTIL THEY BECOME PART OF THE SPECIES. THIS PROCESS CAN TAKE HUNDREDS OR THOUSANDS OF YEARS.

THIS PLANT USES STICKY LIQUID TO CAPTURE AN INSECT, THEN WRAPS AROUND IT. THIS ADAPTATION LIKELY FIRST APPEARED THOUSANDS OF YEARS AGO!

9

OPEN WIDE

The Venus flytrap is a funny-looking plant that looks like it has a big open mouth. Bugs looking for food are drawn to its bright leaves and sticky nectar. But then...snap! The plant traps and eats the bug.

How does it work? The Venus flytrap's leaves are connected by a **hinge**. Tiny hairs covering the leaves sense movement, like a bug crawling on it. In less than a second, the leaves snap shut and its "teeth" keep the bug inside.

CLASSIFIED!
VENUS FLYTRAPS FEED ON ANTS, FLIES, BEETLES, SPIDERS, AND SLUGS. SOME EVEN EAT TINY FROGS!

IT TAKES 5 TO 12 DAYS FOR THE VENUS FLYTRAP TO BREAK DOWN A BUG'S BODY AND ABSORB THE NUTRIENTS. THE PLANT REOPENS WHEN IT'S READY FOR THE NEXT MEAL.

IT'S A TRAP!

This plant is a cobra lily. What's its secret? If you fall inside, you'll never get out! Plenty of bugs learned this the hard way.

The cobra lily has a tricky way to catch prey. Its sweet-smelling nectar encourages bugs to crawl inside. See-through leaves hide the plant's exit, confusing the bug until it gets too tired to fight back. Slippery walls and tiny hairs drag the bug into the plant's base, where **bacteria** help turn it into food.

CLASSIFIED!
THE COBRA LILY USES WHAT'S KNOWN AS A "PITFALL TRAP" TO CATCH PREY.

HOW DID THE COBRA LILY GET ITS NAME? THE PLANT IS SHAPED LIKE A SNAKE WITH A HOODED HEAD, WHILE THE LEAVES LOOK LIKE A MOUTH AND TONGUE.

STICKY SUNDEWS

The carnivorous sundew is brightly colored and covered in special parts that release liquid. The liquid looks like rain or dew drops, which is how the sundew got its name. But those drops are not what they seem. They're really a sticky glue to trap prey!

Bugs land on the sundew and get trapped in the sticky liquid. Then, the plant gets to work. Bit by bit, it squeezes around the bug's body, and slowly breaks it down into food. Yikes!

CLASSIFIED!
IT TAKES 4 TO 6 DAYS FOR A SUNDEW TO **DIGEST** ITS PREY.

THIS BUG GOT TRAPPED BY THE STICKY SUNDEW.

15

PITCHER PLANTS

Pitcher plants are so named because they look like pitchers full of sweet nectar. It's a perfect **lure** for prey looking for a sweet drink. But the prey risks its life if it gets too close. Waiting at the base of the pitcher is a liquid that will turn it into food!

Like the cobra lily, pitcher plants use pitfall traps, hoping that prey will fall inside. Once it does, it can't crawl out of the slippery, deep pitcher.

WHILE MOST CARNIVOROUS PLANTS EAT INSECTS, THE KING OF THE MEAT-EATERS IS THE *NEPENTHES*, A LARGE PITCHER PLANT. IT CAN EAT RATS!

BLADDERWORTS

The bladderwort is a carnivorous plant that grows in water habitats. It has a sneaky secret: a trapdoor to suck in its prey!

Small hairs line the opening of the plant's bladder, which connects to the stem and sits underwater. If prey swimming nearby brushes the hairs, the "door" snaps open. **Pressure** built up behind the door quickly sucks in the water...and the prey with it! The trapdoor closes in less than a second, leaving the prey to its watery grave.

CLASSIFIED!
BLADDERWORTS EAT **LARVAE**, AQUATIC WORMS, AND WATER FLEAS.

ABOVE WATER, THE BLADDERWORT HAS PRETTY FLOWERS. UNDERWATER, IT HAS A BIG APPETITE!

PLANTS ON THE HUNT

Plants are usually thought to be safe, quiet creatures. But now you know their secret: Some of them are hungry predators!

Carnivorous plants' adaptations help them hunt in many ways, from traps set by the Venus flytrap and bladderworts to the pitfall traps used by pitcher plants and cobra lilies. These sneaky methods keep their secret until it's too late for their prey to escape! There's a whole world of carnivorous plants to explore. Are you brave enough to do it?

THIS PLANT'S BRIGHT COLOR AND SWEET LIQUID ATTRACT BUGS... BUT LITTLE DO THEY KNOW WHAT AWAITS THEM!

GLOSSARY

absorb: to take in

attract: to draw nearer

bacteria: tiny creatures that can only be seen with a microscope

digest: to break down food inside the body so that the body can use it

environment: the natural world in which a plant or animal lives

habitat: the natural place where an animal or plant lives

hinge: a place where two things connect that allows them to open and close like a door

larvae: bugs in an early life stage that have a wormlike form. The singular form is "larva."

lure: to draw something closer in order to catch it

nutrient: something a living thing needs to grow and stay alive

pressure: a force that pushes on something else

species: a group of plants or animals that are all of the same kind

FOR MORE INFORMATION

BOOKS
Jones, Keisha. *Plants That Eat.* New York, NY: Powerkids Press, 2017.

Lawler, Janet. *Scary Plants!* New York, NY: Penguin Young Readers, 2017.

Owen, Ruth. *How Do Meat-Eating Plants Catch Their Food?* New York, NY: Powerkids Press, 2015.

WEBSITES

Awesome 8 Carnivorous Plants
hkids.nationalgeographic.com/explore/awesome-8-hub/carnivorous-plants/
Fast facts and colorful pictures bring the world of carnivorous plants to life!

Meat-Eating Plants
kids.nationalgeographic.com/explore/science/meat-eating-plants/
Read fun facts about meat-eating plants.

Meat-Eating Plants
www.dkfindout.com/us/animals-and-nature/plants/meat-eating-plants/
Discover more about plants that eat insects, and see a video of one in action.

Publisher's note to educators and parents: Our editors have carefully reviewed these websites to ensure that they are suitable for students. Many websites change frequently, however, and we cannot guarantee that a site's future contents will continue to meet our high standards of quality and educational value. Be advised that students should be closely supervised whenever they access the internet.

INDEX

adaptation 8, 9, 20
bacteria 12
bladderwort 18, 19, 20
carnivorous plant 6, 17, 18, 20
cobra lily 12, 13, 16, 20
environment 6, 8
habitat 7, 18
insectivore 6
larvae 18
Nepenthes 17

nutrient 6, 7, 8, 11
pitcher plant 16, 17, 20
pitfall trap 12, 16, 20
predator 4, 20
prey 4, 12, 14, 16, 18, 20
species 4
sundew 14, 15
Venus flytrap 10, 11, 20
trapdoor 18